HALO

GREEN PATROL

BEGINNINGS

Written by Bali Rai

Illustrated by Margherita Ende

RISING★STARS

Hachette UK's policy is to use papers that are natural, renewable and recyclable products and made from wood grown in well-managed forests and other controlled sources. The logging and manufacturing processes are expected to conform to the environmental regulations of the country of origin.

ISBN: 9781398324275

Text © 2021 Bali Rai
Illustrations, design and layout © Hodder and Stoughton Ltd
First published in 2021 by Hodder & Stoughton Limited (for its Rising Stars imprint, part of the Hodder Education Group),
An Hachette UK Company
Carmelite House, 50 Victoria Embankment, London EC4Y 0DZ
www.risingstars-uk.com

Impression number 10 9 8 7 6 5 4 3 2 1
Year 2025 2024 2023 2022 2021

Author: Bali Rai
Series Editor: Tony Bradman
Commissioning Editor: Hamish Baxter
Illustrator: Margherita Ende/Astound US
Educational Reviewer: Helen Marron
Design concept: Julie Joubinaux
Page layout: Rocket Design (East Anglia) Ltd
Editor: Amy Tyrer

With thanks to the schools that took part in the development of *Reading Planet* KS2, including: Ancaster CE Primary School, Ancaster; Downsway Primary School, Reading; Ferry Lane Primary School, London; Foxborough Primary School, Slough; Griffin Park Primary School, Blackburn; St Barnabas CE First & Middle School, Pershore; Tranmoor Primary School, Doncaster; and Wilton CE Primary School, Wilton.

A catalogue record for this title is available from the British Library.

Printed in the United Kingdom.

Orders: Please contact Hachette UK Distribution, Hely Hutchinson Centre, Milton Road, Didcot, Oxfordshire, OX11 7HH.

Telephone: (44) 01235 400555. Email: primary@hachette.co.uk.

Chapter 1

Wiston Hall, England ...

Martha looked at a camera screen. The lab was well hidden on a small island, yet robbers had got in.

"There are two of them," said Olive.

Olive was an adult. She looked after Martha. They sat under Wiston Hall, in Martha's command hub.

The lab was set up by Martha's rich mum and dad, but they had disappeared 5 years ago. Martha was 13. She wished to keep doing what they had started – to look after the planet and its animals.

"They must be from TITAN – I bet they are after the eggs!" Martha muttered.

TITAN was a big, rich company. They cut down forests and dumped rubbish in rivers and seas. They harmed the planet to make the company richer. Could it be TITAN that took Martha's mum and dad?

Olive and Martha watched on the camera screen as the two men approached a big, glass tank. It was full of eggs from birds that could soon become extinct.

"They are after the sun parakeet eggs," said Martha.

Sun parakeets were bright, little parrots that were protected by the government.

"Is it something to do with the jobs that HALO are doing in Brazil?" asked Olive.

Martha nodded.

After her mum and dad vanished, Martha took command of their company, called HALO. She was helped by Olive and a handful of children.

HALO was fighting to protect forests and other habitats.

TITAN was cutting down forests in Brazil.

"If we can free a flock of sun parakeets to live in the forests, then TITAN will have to stop cutting down the trees. That will stop their plan to make millions of dollars. TITAN will not like that one bit," said Martha.

"Do we call the gang?" said Olive.

"Yes," said Martha. "And they are *not* just a gang. They are the GREEN PATROL!"

Chapter 2

Brazil ...

Silva's smartwatch
beeped. It was HALO.
He passed the ball to
his friend.

"Got to run!" Silva yelled.

China ...

Shan jumped, dropping her burger. Her
watch buzzed again. It was HALO.

"Clear up that mess!"
yelled the food cart
vendor.

"Sorry!" said Shan as
she sprinted away.

Senegal ...

Ayan sat by the sea with a book.

Her watch buzzed. HALO again.

She jumped up and ran ...

Canada ...

Max's watch buzzed. He pressed a button. "Hello, HALO. Yes, I can hear you," he said.

Wiston Hall, England ...

"Green Patrol, we have a job for you," said Olive, from HALO command. "You will be picked up in 15 mins!"

"What is it?" asked Shan.

"I cannot say," said Olive.

"Oh, Olive, could you tell us?" asked Silva.

"My, my," said Olive. "You do ask a lot!"

"Well, you picked us," said Ayan. "So you can tell us about the job!"

"I did not pick you," said Olive. "Martha did."

Chapter 3

HALO's hidden island ...

Martha grinned at Green Patrol. With all their training and support from HALO, they were all set and keen to get started. No one could suspect a bunch of kids!

"So, what is the job?" Max asked.

"Two robbers took rare birds' eggs from HALO's lab," said Martha.

"Oh, no! I wonder how they discovered the island?" Shan asked.

Martha shrugged.

"But you got them on camera," Ayan added. "So, how did they get away?"

"I let them," said Martha.

"You let them?" asked Silva.

"It's OK. I am watching them," said Martha.

"So, you wish to get the eggs back?" asked Max.

"No," said Martha. "For now, we just track the eggs."

"And how far away are they now?" asked Shan.

"They are in Jamaica," said Martha. "Ever been?"

Chapter 4

Jamaica ...

Green Patrol landed at a hidden HALO airstrip. It was midday and very hot. The hills were lush with trees and bushes.

"Wow!" said Ayan. "It is stunning."

Olive took a tablet out of her bag. "Here," she said, "have a look."

They were looking at a report marked **'FOR HALO EYES ONLY'**.

"The target is John Redmond," Martha said. "He is part of TITAN."

JOHN REDMOND

FOR HALO EYES ONLY

"How come he steals rare eggs?" asked Max. "He is mega rich!"

"The eggs are protected. You cannot collect, steal or sell them. We suspect he steals rare animals, too," Martha told him.

"So, how come you have them?" asked Shan.

"We are allowed to. HALO protects animals," said Martha. "It was all part of Mum and Dad's plan until they ..."

Olive cut in as she could see that Martha was getting upset. "We have tracked the signal for the parakeet eggs. They are in the animal park, and it shuts at 3p.m."

Martha shed a tear. This was no time to be sad.

"Shan and Silva, come with me," said Martha. "Max and Ayan, you are with Olive."

Max and Ayan fist bumped and Shan and Silva did high tens.

"Right, we must go!" said Olive.

Chapter 5

Ayan and Max went to the animal park with Olive. It was packed but cooler under the trees.

"That is better," said Max. "It was too hot."

"Stop moaning," Ayan told him.

Two paths forked left and right.

"You have phones," said Olive. "Turn them on. Look for the map with the tracking signal."

The phones were ultra-thin. No buttons –
just a screen.

"Never seen a phone like this ..."
muttered Max.

"Cool," said Ayan.

"Keep it in your hand so you can see the
map. You two go left.
I will go right," said
Olive. "Track the
signal for the eggs
on the map. Put
your ear buds in.
You can now hear
the rest of us,
and we can
hear you."

"What are we looking for?" asked Max.

"We are just back-up for the rest of the gang," said Olive. "But stay alert!"

Martha, Shan and Silva were up in the hills. They were looking at John Redmond's big house.

"Swimming pool, helicopter landing pad … wow!" said Silva.

Martha had a map of the house.

"Here," she said, tapping the screen. "We creep down and go in. The staff will be on lunch. Now, off we go!"

ANIMAL PARK

Chapter 6

Mr Redmond's house on the hill ...

Shan and Silva made no noise as they crept about the house. Martha stayed in the gardens, on look out.

"The stairs go down to a corridor," Martha said in their ear buds.

"What next?" asked Shan.

"The door at the end has a scanner pad," said Martha. "Put your phone to it."

As soon as Shan held out her phone, the door unlocked.

"Now, can you see a steel door?" asked Martha. "Put Shan's phone up to it again."

When the second door opened, they saw more stairs. They led down to a lit tunnel.

"We can feel fresh air," Shan said.

"It's a cave complex," said Martha. "What can you hear?"

Shan and Silva stopped. "Animals!" they said.

"I can smell them, too," Silva frowned.

The tunnel led to a big, well-lit cave. The cave was full of hundreds of animals in metal pens. There were white tigers, black panthers, orangutans, gorillas and much more.

"Oh, no!" sighed Silva.

"Is that a Komodo dragon?" asked Shan.

"Yes, yes, it is!" said someone from the darkness ...

A well-dressed man appeared. He had two big men with him.

"I am John Redmond. What are you prowling about for?" he demanded.

Shan looked at Silva and Silva looked at Shan, their eyes full of fear.

Chapter 7

Back at the animal park ...

Ayan and Max could hear what was going on in their ear buds. Shan and Silva needed help!

"We need to distract the men, now!" Martha yelled.

A red dot flashed up on Max and Ayan's tracking map. It was Olive.

"Get here fast!" she hissed. They spotted Olive by the chimpanzees.

"I can think of something to help Shan and Silva," said Ayan. "Can we hack into the park's computers?"

"Here, Ayan," said Olive. She took a small tablet from her backpack.

"What are you doing?" asked Max.

"Tricking the park's computer," said Ayan. "I'm linking it to HALO's computer. Now we can tell it what to do."

"What for?" said Max.

"To make a fuss," said Olive.

Max looked at the animals. "Oh," he grinned. "I get it!"

Ayan tapped the screen. Several of the animals' pens opened. The animals scampered out and ran for freedom.

"YES!" yelled Ayan.

"You *are* good!" said Max.

Ayan tapped the screen again. The park alarm went off.

"Oh, dear," said Olive. "What did you do?"

Ayan just grinned.

Chapter 8

In the cave under Mr Redmond's house ...

"Komodo dragons," hissed John Redmond with a horrid grin. "All with 60 razor-sharp teeth ..."

In its metal pen, one of them flicked its forked tongue. It could smell them. Shan shivered, and Silva's teeth began to chatter. The big men held them so they could not get away.

"But I'm no monster," said Redmond. "Tell me which person sent you and I will let you go."

"Never," said Shan.

"I think you will tell," said Redmond.
"Or your friend will meet my monster
lizard ..."

"No!" wailed Shan.

Silva began to fight back, but the big man
was too strong.

"Feet!" yelled Shan.

Silva stamped on the man's foot.
He howled and let go.

"Get him!" ordered Redmond.

All of a sudden, an alarm went off.

"What is that?"

"It's an alert at the park, Mr Redmond!"
said one of the men.

Chapter 9

At the animal park, a cop car pulled up. Three cops jumped out. The park keepers had got all the animals back in their pens.

"What now?" Max asked.

"We wait …" said Olive.

A thundering noise filled the air as a helicopter zoomed past and landed next to the big house.

"Just in time," said Olive.

Down in the cave, John Redmond was panicking.

"Bring those brats back to the house and lock them up."

Redmond's men grabbed Shan and Silva. Redmond led the way. All of a sudden he stopped ...

... and Martha appeared. She stepped into the cave. "Mr Redmond," she said.

"What?" he gasped. *"You?"*

Martha held up her phone.

"I have you on camera, frightening children with big lizards," she said. "And what you are doing is criminal."

Redmond sneered. "If I just took the phone," he said. "You could not stop me."

"Too bad," said Martha. "I have

filmed it and sent it to HALO command."

"I will never let you go. Give up now, or ..."

Redmond stopped. His cheeks turned red with anger.

A man stood next to Martha.

"Hello, Inspector Smith," said Martha.

"This is a set up!" complained Redmond.

The inspector shook his head as he handcuffed him. "John Redmond, I am arresting you for putting children at risk and stealing rare animals," he said.

"You meddling brats!" yelled Redmond as he was dragged away.

Chapter 10

Wiston Hall, England ...

"What is next?" Silva asked Martha.

"Redmond is finished," said Martha. "We stopped his main plan, and those animals that were in the cave are now protected."

"What main plan?" asked Max. "The eggs?"

Martha nodded. "Yes, they were for TITAN," she grinned. "To stop the job we are doing next in Brazil."

"Brazil?" said Silva. "That is where I am from!"

"But we have just got back!" said Ayan.
"I want to chill and have pizza ..."

Martha grinned. "This is Green Patrol,"
she said. "We never stop. And we *never
give up!*"

Chat about the book

1 Go to Chapter 1. What were the robbers after?

2 Look at page 13. Look at how 'FOR HALO EYES ONLY' has been written. What effect does this have?

3 Go to page 25. 'Shan shivered, and Silva's teeth began to chatter.' What does this tell us?

4 How is the start and end of the book similar?

5 Look at page 31. Martha says, "We never stop. And we *never give up*." What do you think will happen next?

6 Do you think Green Patrol do an important job? Explain.